Gwyneth Rees

The Butterfly Tiara

Illustrated by Jessie Eckel

MACMILLAN CHILDREN'S BOOKS

For my darling girls Eliza and Lottie

First published 2012 by Macmillan Children's Books
a division of Macmillan Publishers Limited
20 New Wharf Road, London N1 9RR
Basingstoke and Oxford
Associated companies throughout the world
www.panmacmillan.com

ISBN 978-0-330-46118-4

Text copyright © Gwyneth Rees 2012
Illustrations copyright © Jessie Eckel 2012

The right of Gwyneth Rees and Jessie Eckel to be identified as the
author and illustrator of this work has been asserted by them in accordance
with the Copyright, Designs and Patents Act 1988.

1 3 5 7 9 8 6 4 2

A CIP catalogue record for this book is available from
the British Library.

Printed and bound by CPI Group (UK) Ltd, Croydon CR0 4YY

1

'Where are we travelling to today, Marietta?'
Ava asked her aunt, hardly able to contain
her excitement as she bounded inside
Marietta's magic dress shop.

'Somewhere very exciting, Ava,' Marietta
replied, smiling. 'Now . . . what do you
think of my outfit?'

Marietta was wearing a pair of red, light-
as-a-feather, silk flared trousers that had a
fluffy trim around each ankle. Above this she
wore a red halter-neck top that was totally
covered in silver spangles. Her long wavy
hair was piled up in a bun on top of her

1

head and on her feet she wore a pair of sparkly silver pumps. 'You look amazing, Marietta! Are you dressed as a dancer?'

'Something like that,' Marietta replied, grinning.

Ava could hardly believe how much her life had changed since she'd come to stay with her father for the summer holidays two weeks earlier, while her mum went away sailing. She certainly didn't feel like the same nine-year-old girl who had arrived

2

at her dad's house with no knowledge of Marietta's magic dress shop or of the extraordinary truth about Dad's family.

'This will be the chance you've always wanted to get to know your dad better,' her mum had said, for Ava had spent very little time with her father since her parents had split up when she was just a baby.

'I *hope* so,' Ava had replied uncertainly, because much as she wanted to be closer to her dad, he had always seemed a bit distant and difficult to chat to whenever they'd got together in the past.

It was only now that Ava had learned the secret her dad had been keeping from her for all this time – a secret that even Mum didn't know. Ava's father came from a long line of people who were able to travel via magic portals to other times and places,

3

both real and imaginary. The portals existed in the form of magic mirrors – of which Marietta had many in her shop – and people with this special gift could travel through them if they were wearing the right magic clothes. The exciting thing was that Ava could do it too.

The whole thing had been almost impossible to believe at first – until Ava had experienced the magic for herself. So far she had travelled through two magic portals – the first had led her to the fairy-tale land of Cinderella and the second had taken her backwards in time to Victorian London. Now she was to make her third journey with Marietta, who was going to be looking after her while her dad spent the weekend working.

Marietta's wide-bottomed trousers flapped

 4

breezily about her ankles as she led the way through the ordinary front section of the shop into the secret warren of rooms at the back.

The first room was one Ava was very familiar with by now, but that didn't stop her feeling a tingle of pleasure as she looked around at the walls, which were all painted with colourful scenes from different fairy tales. The room contained dozens of beautiful gowns fit for a princess to wear and had a whole wall of shelves that displayed fairy-tale accessories – everything from crowns and tiaras to Cinderella-style glass slippers. In the centre of the room was a gold spiral staircase that led both upwards and downwards. Ava had already been to the room at the top of the staircase – which housed Marietta's fairy-tale wedding

5

collection – but she had yet to visit the basement below.

'Since we've got the whole weekend together I thought it would be fun to go back in time by sixty years and visit a travelling circus,' Marietta said. 'That's why I'm wearing this – it's from my circus-costume collection.'

'Oh . . .' Ava frowned uncertainly, thinking of what her mother had told her about traditional circuses of the past, with their animal acts such as dancing bears, tigers jumping through burning hoops and elephants parading around the ring trunk-to-tail.

'What's wrong?' Marietta asked in surprise. 'Don't you like that idea?'

'It's just . . .' Ava began, flushing a little. 'It's just . . . my mum told me that the

 6

animals in those circuses were really badly treated. She said they were forced to learn tricks that they didn't really want to do, and that they must have been really unhappy.'

Marietta nodded. 'That's why the circus I'm taking you to visit is a strictly *non*-animal one. There are acrobats, trapeze artists, clowns, contortionists, fire-eaters, knife-throwers, sword-swallowers – but definitely no animals.'

Ava felt relieved as Marietta led her down the gold spiral staircase. And at the bottom she forgot everything else as she stood open-mouthed in awe. The large basement room was entirely round – just like a circus ring – and brightly lit by a large spotlight in the ceiling. A red-and-gold-painted border represented the barrier around the ring and, above this, a huge mural curved its way

7

round the room. The mural showed rows and rows of faces getting smaller and smaller as they rose upward, creating the impression of an audience on tiered seating.

In the middle of the room a long, flexible clothes rack displayed dozens of colourful circus costumes. There were red-and-black ringmaster's jackets, clown costumes of every bright colour and bold pattern imaginable, and a multitude of sequinned leotards and glittering bodysuits. There were regal-looking capes, brightly coloured sequinned shirts, flashy showbiz-style dresses decorated in spangles and sparkles, richly embroidered gold tunics, velvet waistcoats and baggy silk trousers. Most beautiful of all, however, were the exotic corset-and-feathers bird costumes and the butterfly costumes with their large wings of richly painted silk that stretched from wrist to ankle.

'Wow!' Ava gasped.

Marietta laughed. 'I was hoping you'd say that.' As she spoke she beckoned for Ava to follow her through a small arched opening in the wall, which led to a room that resembled a performers' changing area. It contained a typical backstage dressing table with a mirror surrounded by light bulbs, two or three full-length mirrors propped up against the walls, and several large, brightly painted wooden storage trunks.

The huge trunk nearest to Ava was labelled CLOWN ACCESSORIES and Ava lifted the lid expecting to find an exciting jumble of different things. Instead everything was arranged neatly and methodically in separate compartments. There were shiny red noses, plastic flower brooches that

 10

squirted out water, curly clown wigs in
multiple colours, huge neck ruffles, spotty
bow ties, several silly hats and a pair of
oversized and ridiculous clown shoes.

'Oh, it must be great fun to dress up as a
clown!' Ava exclaimed in delight, holding a
red nose to her face and grinning at herself
in the mirror that was fixed to the inside lid
of the trunk.

'You're welcome to borrow anything that's here,' Marietta said. 'There's some clown make-up somewhere and I can paint your face for you if you like. But you might want to have a proper look at all the other costumes first. All the children's clothes are out there on the rack.'

Dad was coming down the spiral staircase with Ava's overnight bag as they stepped back outside. 'I thought I heard voices down here. Ava, what do you think of Marietta's circus collection then?'

'It's wonderful!' Ava exclaimed.

'I thought you'd like it.' He paused. 'Ava, I want you to have a good time this weekend, but I don't want you wandering off on your own when you get to the other side of the portal. Understood?' As Ava nodded obediently, he turned to his sister.

'I'm trusting you to keep a close eye on her, Marietta.'

'Of course, Otto,' Marietta reassured him, used to her older brother's protectiveness when it came to matters of time-travelling.

'Good . . . well . . .' He leaned towards Ava as if he might be going to kiss her goodbye, but ended up looking self-conscious and patting her awkwardly on the arm instead. 'Have fun and I'll see you tomorrow.'

'Bye, Dad,' Ava said, wanting to let him know that it would be fine if he gave her a kiss – that with her mother kisses and hugs were just a normal part of everyday life. But too soon the moment had passed.

'Come on, Ava,' Marietta said, giving her shoulders a squeeze as they watched him leave. 'It's time we got you changed into some magic clothes!'

2

When Marietta showed her the children's clothes, Ava couldn't decide what she most wanted to wear. Then she saw one costume that made her feel quite tingly with excitement.

'Please can I try this on?' she asked Marietta, pointing to a particularly amazing multicoloured butterfly outfit.

'Of course,' Marietta replied, smiling. 'I'll help you.'

The costume consisted of a long-sleeved, purple-sequinned leotard, a pair of boldly patterned red-and-orange wings, sparkly

 14

gold tights,
purple ballet
pumps and the
most beautiful
tiara Ava had
ever seen.

'Wow!' Ava
gasped as she
held the tiara reverently in both hands. 'It
looks like it belongs to a princess.'

The tiara's shiny gold band was decorated
at the front with a magnificent butterfly
made from a stunning mosaic of red,
purple and orange glittering jewels which
Marietta told her would become real rubies,
amethysts and rare orange diamonds on the
other side of the magic mirror.

'The Butterfly Tiara is very special,'
Marietta told her. 'It reacts by glowing more

15

brightly when a person with the travelling gift puts it on.' She sighed wistfully as she added, 'It was one of my mother's favourite pieces.'

Ava's grandparents had disappeared twelve years earlier, leaving a letter to say that they had gone to live in a particular fantasy land they had discovered. They hadn't been heard from since, but Ava knew that both her aunt and her father hoped to see them again one day.

Ava quickly changed into the leotard and tights and let Marietta help her with the wings, which hooked on over the shoulders and were made from the same transparent satin netting Ava had seen before on ballet tutus.

'Now the tiara,' Marietta said, holding it up.

 16

Ava felt a thrill run through her, for this was the part of the costume that excited her the most. After Marietta had fixed it on to her head, Ava reached up delicately to touch it. As she looked at herself in the long mirror attached to one end of the clothes rack she couldn't help thinking how stunning she looked. And Marietta was right – the tiara on her head did seem to be shining even more brightly.

'I feel like the Queen of the Butterflies,'
she told Marietta, smiling.

'You look absolutely gorgeous!' Marietta
declared. 'This trapeze costume might have
been made for you.'

'*Trapeze* costume?' Ava queried in surprise.
She reached back to touch her wings,
wondering how such an outfit could possibly
be worn safely in a flying trapeze act.

'Oh, the wings are only for show when
you first enter the ring,' Marietta explained
quickly. 'It's the same as those fancy capes
trapeze artists wear. They take them off
before they do their act. My costume comes
with a cape, and both it and these trousers
would be left on the ground I should think.'
She laughed at the horrified look on Ava's
face. 'Don't worry, I'd still be quite decent.
Look.' She undid a clip on the side of the

18

trousers and revealed that her own sparkly
top was in fact a leotard, and that under
the wrap-around trousers she wore silver-
coloured tights. 'Now . . .' She went over
to the rack and picked up a long, red, silver-
lined cape that matched the rest of her outfit
perfectly.

'So which mirror is the magic one?' Ava
asked as she watched Marietta fasten the
cape.

'Let's see if you can guess,' Marietta said,
leading her back into the changing room.

Ava rushed straight over to the mirror
surrounded by light bulbs. Convinced it
must be the magic one, she stared into it,
concentrating as hard as she could on her
reflection, waiting for the magic reaction
to start up. But to her surprise nothing
happened.

19

'Remember that the magic mirror isn't always the most obvious one,' Marietta reminded her.

Ava thought about the two mirrors she had travelled through previously. One had seemed a very obvious choice among the others in the room. The other however had taken her a while to find because it hadn't even been in plain view to start off with . . .

Ava slowly went over to the trunk of clown accessories and opened the lid again.

The rectangular mirror inside looked rusty at the edges as if it had been there a very long time. A tingle of anticipation ran through her as she inspected it. '*This* is the one, isn't it?'

Marietta smiled. 'I was twelve when I discovered this particular portal. I'd been invited to a fancy-dress party and I thought I'd go as a clown. I was using this mirror to put on my clown make-up when I suddenly felt the magic starting up. That's how I found myself visiting a nineteen-thirties travelling circus – and meeting Tony!'

'Tony?'

'Yes. On the other side of the mirror I met a boy my own age – the nephew of the circus owner. It's the early nineteen fifties there now and he's grown up too – and he's got his own trapeze act. I've been back to see him quite a few times over the years. Recently he's been teaching me some tricks on the trapeze and he says I might even perform in the show with him after I've had a bit more practice.'

'Really?' Ava was impressed.

'Yes, but I haven't told your dad. You know how overprotective he gets. Now . . . if you're ready, let's set off. Shall I go first?'

Ava nodded, watching as her aunt knelt down in front of the trunk so that it was easier to look into the mirror.

It wasn't long before something started to happen. First came the gentle glow that signalled the start of the magic reaction, at which point Marietta's red hair began to glow too. Very quickly, the whole room became flooded with light – a dazzling, blindingly bright light that forced Ava to shut her eyes.

Only when the brightness had subsided did Ava look again – by which time Marietta was gone.

Now it was Ava's turn. She too knelt
down and gazed at her reflection in the
mirror as her aunt had done until, after a few
seconds, the mirror started to respond. The
longer Ava stayed there, the more the magic
reaction took hold. Ava's head felt swimmy
and her pulse was racing as she closed her
eyes against the glare. And this time when
she opened her eyes again, her heart skipped
a beat as she saw
that the magic
had worked
for her too.

Ava found herself inside some sort of small caravan, seated at a bulky, rather ugly old-fashioned dressing table with a matching swivel-style mirror that had photos and coloured postcards stuck around its edge. Ava's reflection in the mirror made her gasp, for the butterfly on her tiara looked even more stunning on this side of the portal now that the jewels were real.

She looked around her and saw that the walls were decorated with yellow-and-blue floral wallpaper, and that blue polka-dot curtains hung at the windows. The narrow

 24

bed, which clearly doubled as a sofa, was covered with a bubblegum-pink fluffy throw and scattered with round zebra-striped cushions. In the other half of the caravan she saw a very small fifties-style dining booth with blue leather seats and a shiny formica-topped table.

Ava quickly located the door and stepped outside. The caravan was a small yellow one with a domed roof, on the side of which – in large fancy lettering – were the words: PRINCESS STELLA, CONTORTIONIST AND ESCAPOLOGIST EXTRAORDINAIRE.

It was parked in a large field along with several other caravans, lorries, trailers and tents. At the other end of the field, taking up a massive space, was a gigantic round red-and-yellow tent with a high peaked roof.

'The circus big top!' Ava exclaimed in delight.

Marietta was standing a short distance away, exchanging enthusiastic hugs with a girl of Ava's age who was dressed in an exotic Indian maharaja-style costume.

'Ava, this is Lexi,' Marietta said as Ava joined them. 'Her family owns the circus.'

'Hi,' Lexi said, smiling at her. 'I love your tiara!'

'Thanks,' Ava said shyly. 'I love your turban!'

Lexi laughed and put up her hand to touch her gold silk turban, which was decorated at the front with a large peacock feather. The rest of her outfit was also very grand – a red-and-gold embroidered tunic, a pair of gold baggy silk trousers with elastic around the ankles and a pair of gold curl-toe slippers.

'So why are you dressed like that, Lexi?' Marietta asked now.

Lexi pulled a face. 'Uncle Max has decided I'm going to be his new elephant rider – at least for the publicity photographs. He says I'll look really sweet sitting astride his new baby elephant.'

'But I thought—'

'That we were a strictly *non*-animal circus,' Lexi finished for her. 'I know, but everything's changed since Dad's been in hospital. Uncle Max is in charge now, and he's decided we ought to have animal acts like all the other circuses.'

'Wait a minute . . . your father's in hospital?'

'He went in three weeks ago to have his appendix out and something went wrong while they were operating. He's been in intensive care ever since.'

'Oh, Lexi, I'm so sorry!' Marietta exclaimed. 'Is your mum with him?'

Lexi nodded. 'Uncle Max had to move

the circus on without him, so Mum's staying in a guest house close to the hospital so she can visit Dad every day. She says we've to keep thinking positive despite what the doctors say.' Lexi's voice quavered slightly as she added, 'They keep telling us to prepare ourselves for the worst, but Mum doesn't want to. Mum says he's going to be fine.'

'Oh . . . well . . . of course . . .' Marietta looked distressed.

'I keep saying that to Uncle Max. I keep telling him Dad's going to be fine and that he's going to be furious when he comes out of hospital and finds out about Sukey.'

'Sukey?' Marietta queried.

'That's what we've called the baby elephant. She's ever so sweet. I'm going there now to have my photo taken with her if you want to come and see.'

29

'Why don't *you* go, Ava, while I go and find Tony?' Marietta suggested.

'I can show you round the rest of the circus afterwards if you like, Ava,' Lexi offered.

'Really?'

'Oh yes. I haven't got anything to do for the rest of the morning – and I can't stand being bored.'

'Well, thanks – that would be great,' Ava said with a smile.

Lexi smiled too. 'OK then. Follow me.'

'Tony will be over the moon to see Marietta.' Lexi chatted as they walked past a couple of old buses that had their side windows covered with frilly curtains. 'The twins will be furious though.'

'The twins?'

 30

'My cousins, Dulcie and Gemma. They're not really twins – Gemma's sixteen and Dulcie's seventeen – but Uncle Max thinks "Tony and the Trapeze Twins" sounds better on the programme. They're really spoilt and they're dead jealous of Marietta.'

'Why?' Ava asked in surprise.

'Because she's much prettier than them and because they know Tony prefers working with her.'

Ava was about to ask if Marietta came here a lot to practise on the trapeze with Tony, when they arrived at the edge of the field, where a big lorry was standing a little apart from the other vehicles. With its long bonnet and huge headlamps it looked more old-fashioned than the lorries Ava was used to. The upper flap of the lorry's rear door was propped open and to Ava's

31

astonishment they could hear weeping coming from inside.

'Oh . . .' was all Ava could manage to say after they had climbed into the back.

Huddled in one corner of the lorry was a baby elephant. It had light grey skin, a cute little wrinkly trunk, big floppy ears, a tuft of wispy hair on top of its head – and very sad eyes. Tears were running down its face as it continued to make the same heart-wrenching crying noise.

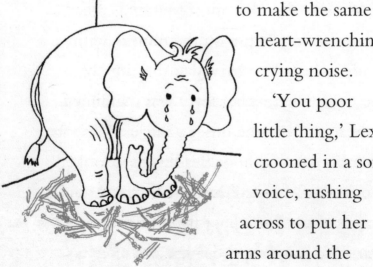

'You poor little thing,' Lexi crooned in a soft voice, rushing across to put her arms around the

animal. 'You miss your mother, don't you?'
She looked up at Ava. 'She's been here a
week and she's been crying on and off like
this the whole time.'

'I didn't know elephants *could* cry,' Ava
murmured.

'Oh yes. They cry real saltwater tears
when they get upset, just like we do.
Elephants are a lot like us really. Dad told
me that in the wild baby elephants live in
families, and if a baby in the herd is upset
the entire family goes to comfort it.'

'Poor Sukey – you must be *so* lonely
and frightened right now!' Ava exclaimed,
moving closer to gently lay her hand on the
animal's side. 'So where *is* her mother?'

'Uncle Max says he doesn't know – not
that I believe him. It's easy to tell when he's
lying, because he gets all red and fidgety.'

Lexi frowned. 'Oh, Sukey . . . I wish we could help you.'

As Ava started to stroke Sukey's head the elephant turned to look at her. Sukey seemed to be looking right into her eyes. Then she gave a little whimper and brushed the end of her trunk against Ava's hand as if she recognized Ava as a friend.

'Wow – it took me ages to get her to trust me,' Lexi murmured.

'Hey, have you seen my dad?' came a sudden sharp voice from outside and both girls looked up to see a scowly teenager with a freckled face and blonde curly hair peering into the back of the lorry at them.

'Gemma!' Lexi exclaimed. 'I thought you and Dulcie were practising your act with Tony?'

'Tony's girlfriend has just arrived,'

Gemma grumbled. 'That's why I want to speak to Dad. Tony shouldn't be wasting his time with Marietta when he's supposed to be practising with *us*.'

Ava immediately felt indignant on Marietta's behalf. 'Marietta *isn't* his girlfriend!' she said hotly. 'And *she* needs to practise too if Tony's going to put her in his show!'

'In the *show*?' Gemma looked shocked. 'You're kidding!'

Lexi looked amused as she told her cousin, 'Ava is Marietta's niece, by the way.'

Gemma's face went bright red. 'Well, you'd better tell your show-off auntie to watch her back from now on,' she snapped at Ava. 'The

trapeze is no place to make enemies!' And
with that she stormed off.

'What does she mean?' asked Ava, feeling
nervous all of a sudden. 'They wouldn't do
anything to *hurt* Marietta, would they?'

Before Lexi could answer they heard
Gemma's voice complaining loudly to
somebody outside. Shortly afterwards the
back door of the lorry opened again and a
scowling middle-aged man in trousers and
red braces hauled himself inside.

'Hello, Uncle Max,' Lexi said cheerfully.
'This is Ava. She's Marietta's niece.'

'I know who she is,' he grunted. 'What I
want to know is what does she think she's
doing upsetting my Gemma like that?' Max
turned to confront Ava, but did a double
take as he saw her tiara. 'Cor blimey, girl!' he
exclaimed instead. 'Are those jewels for *real*?'

4

Fortunately Max's attention was quickly
diverted away from the tiara as a younger
man leaped into the lorry behind him.

'This is Tommy, our new elephant
trainer.' Max
introduced
him as Sukey
took a few
nervous steps
backwards.

'Let's 'ave
a look at
'er then!'

Tommy said, boldly approaching the elephant, who began to swipe at him angrily with her trunk. 'Feisty, are we?' said Tommy as he dodged out of her way. 'Well, don't worry . . . we'll soon knock that out of you!'

'You're not going to hurt her, are you?' Lexi asked in alarm.

'Be quiet, Lexi,' snapped her uncle. 'He knows what he's doing.'

Tommy looked from Lexi to Ava, then back again. 'An elephant rider and a butterfly trapeze girl, eh? Well, ain't that swell!' He too stared long and hard at Ava's tiara, letting out a low whistle before turning back to Lexi's uncle. 'I'll need these kids to stay away from the animal from now on. We don't want them being too soft on her. The faster we break her spirit the better.'

Max nodded. 'Off you go, children. Oh . . . and the photographer from the paper can't come until tomorrow, so you can change out of that costume, Lexi.'

'What does he mean – break Sukey's spirit?' Ava whispered as soon as they were outside.

'I'm not sure. Let's listen,' Lexi replied, creeping back to stand as close as possible to the open rear door of the lorry.

'How long will it take to train her?' Max was asking Tommy. 'I've my brother to think of, see. If he *does* pull through – which doesn't seem likely, but you never know – I need the act drawing in the crowds by the time he gets out of hospital.'

'It shouldn't take too long with a baby as young as this,' Tommy told him, 'as long as you're not too squeamish about how you go about it. In my experience a good jab with a pitchfork soon lets 'em know who's boss. Electric shocks tend to do the trick as well. Just leave it to me. I can start tomorrow.'

Ava let out a little gasp of horror and turned to look at Lexi.

Lexi had gone pale. 'We've got to get Sukey out of here,' she whispered hoarsely.

'Yes . . .' Ava agreed. 'Could we phone the RSPCA or something?'

Lexi's lip was trembling as she shook her head. 'My uncle will say we're making it up if we tell anybody. Oh, Ava . . . if only my dad would get better . . .' And she burst into tears.

★

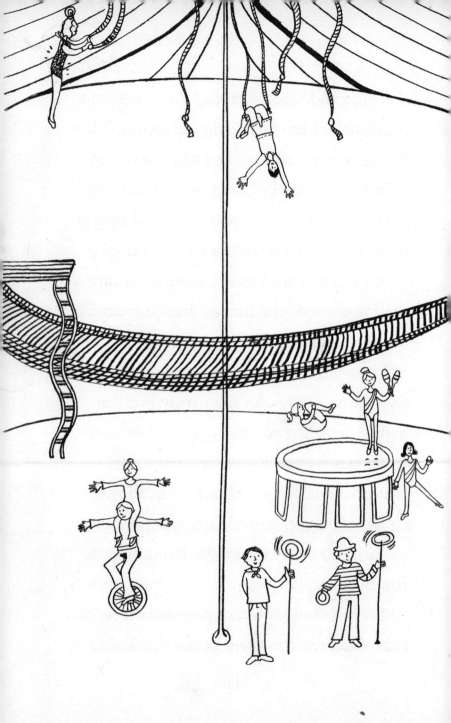

'Let's go and find Marietta,' Ava suggested gently when Lexi had stopped crying. 'She might know how we can help Sukey.'

But inside the big top a lot seemed to be happening and Ava saw that it wasn't going to be easy to get Marietta's attention.

A variety of performers were practising their acts inside the ring at the same time. A young man was riding on a unicycle while a girl in a pink sparkly catsuit balanced on his shoulders. Two older men were practising a plate-spinning act and a group of girls in leotards were practising somersaults on a trampoline while juggling balls in the air.

'Marietta's up there.' Lexi was pointing up towards the roof, where the flying trapeze had been rigged. Various ropes hung down and across from different places and a large safety net was strung up under the whole

area. A long rope ladder led up to a narrow
platform, where Ava could see Marietta in
her red sparkly leotard and tights standing
holding the trapeze bar in one hand.

'That's Tony,' Lexi said, pointing to a
dark-haired young man who was hanging
by his knees from another trapeze swing,
shouting across to Marietta and clapping his
hands together at the same time.

Ava watched open-mouthed as Marietta
took off from the platform, swinging
herself through the air towards Tony.
Tony caught her by the wrists and they
swung to and fro together a couple of
times before Tony launched Marietta back
into the air with a twist and she caught the
empty bar.

'She's done that loads of times before,'
Lexi reassured Ava, seeing her shocked face.

'And anyway, there's always the net if she misses. Shall we call up to them?'

Ava shook her head, reckoning that, despite the net, it was better to leave Marietta to concentrate on what she was doing. 'Let's come back and speak to them later.'

'OK,' Lexi agreed. 'Let's go and find Stella instead. She always knows everything that's going on.'

'Do you mean *Princess* Stella, the contortionist?' Ava asked, remembering the writing on the side of the caravan that housed the magic mirror.

'That's right, though the "Princess" bit is just for the act of course.' Lexi led Ava out through a flap in the side of the big top, adding, 'She likes practising outside, away from the others. Look, there she is!'

Lexi was pointing to a slim young woman in a purple catsuit who was balancing upside down on her hands, her body bent over backwards so far that the back of her head was touching her bottom.

'Wow!' Ava gasped.

'That's nothing,' Lexi told her. 'In the show she does that *and* shoots a bow and arrow with her feet. She never misses the target either. Dad says she's one of the best back-benders he knows.'

'Hi, girls,' said Stella, unfolding herself

from her impossible-looking pose.

'Stella, this is Marietta's niece – Ava,' Lexi said quickly.

Stella smiled and extended her hand. 'Oh, is Marietta visiting us again? Seems like we can't keep her and Tony apart these days! Hello, Ava – nice to meet you. Wow, what an amazing tiara!'

'Thanks,' Ava said, flushing a little.

'Stella, we were wondering if you know anything about the baby elephant Uncle Max just bought—' Lexi began.

'It's terrible, isn't it?' Stella interrupted her at once. 'The reason I joined this circus was because there are *no* animal acts. Your grandfather always wanted it that way and so did your dad, but not Max . . .' She sighed. 'I know the two of them have never got on very well, but I just can't believe Max has

done this *now*, when your dad is . . .' She trailed off, but they both knew what she meant.

'Stella, do you have *any* idea where Sukey came from?' Lexi asked her.

Stella shook her head. 'When I asked Max he told me it was none of my business. All I've heard is that a lorry – not one of ours – arrived in the middle of the night about a week ago with the baby elephant inside.'

Lexi frowned, lowering her voice. 'Stella . . . you don't think Sukey could be *stolen*, do you?'

Stella sighed. 'It's crossed my mind . . . what with Max refusing to say where he got her. Though how he expects to get away with it if she *is* stolen I really don't know!'

'Maybe we should go online and see if a baby elephant has been reported missing

47

from anywhere recently,' Ava suggested helpfully.

'Go on *what* line?' Lexi asked, looking confused.

'Nothing,' Ava mumbled, quickly realizing her mistake. Obviously the Internet hadn't been invented sixty years ago. How weird it must be to live without it, she thought.

'Listen, girls, even if Sukey *was* stolen we can't just accuse Max without any proof,' Stella said.

'But, Stella, we've got to do *something*,' Lexi insisted. 'Sukey's just a baby and she needs her mum. And that elephant trainer sounds really cruel. We have to get Sukey away from him.'

Stella frowned. 'Tell you what . . . If you find out for sure that Sukey's been

 48

stolen then I'll help you.'

'Thanks, Stella,' Lexi said, cheering up. 'Come on, Ava. I'd better get out of this costume. Then let's go and see what we can find out from Uncle Max!'

5

'Uncle Max and Aunt Val do a knife-throwing act together,' Lexi said as she led the way to their caravan, having stopped off on the way to get changed. 'She's his human target.'

'Isn't she scared he'll really hit her?' Ava asked in awe.

Lexi laughed. 'Aunt Val isn't scared of anything . . . oh . . . except spiders! Once a spider crawled on to her foot while she was leaving the stage after her act and she just about screamed the place down. The audience thought it was hilarious.'

As they approached the caravan they heard raised voices and Lexi whispered, 'That's them. They must be round the back practising. Follow me.'

The two girls peered around the corner of the caravan to see Max standing with a knife in his hand, ready to throw it at Val, who was leaning against a huge target-board, her arms and legs splayed out as if she was waiting for someone to draw around her.

'You can't lie to me, Max,' she snapped as he threw the first knife. She didn't even flinch as it landed beside her right ankle. 'I know there's something going on! If you *did* steal that elephant I hope you've covered your tracks, that's all I can say.' She waited for the second knife to land before adding, 'And whatever you've done you were a fool to keep me out of it. You're hopeless at doing anything on your own.'

'I wanted to protect you.' Max stuck up for himself hotly as he prepared to throw a third knife. 'I thought the less you knew the better – especially if my brother *does* pull through.'

'Yes, well, you'd better pray that he

doesn't! Those doctors said he wouldn't last a week after his operation and he's still with us. He's a tough one, Max, and you were a fool to think otherwise!'

Ava glanced at Lexi, but she didn't seem too upset – or surprised – to hear them talking like this about her dad.

Max looked furious and Ava held her breath as he took out two more knives and threw them both at Val in quick succession, the blades skimming each of her earlobes to land perfectly on either side of her head.

'Where's that paper you were reading the other day – the one you wouldn't let me see?' Val demanded.

Max sounded defensive. 'I don't know what you mean.'

'Oh yes you do! When I asked you what you were doing with a local rag from up north you went all red and squirmy on me.'

The two of them went on bickering until Val finally abandoned their practice session and stormed off in a rage. Max was left to mutter angrily to himself as he collected up his knives and went back inside their caravan. Ava and Lexi were about to leave too when Max suddenly stepped outside again. He was holding a folded newspaper.

They followed him, staying as close behind as they dared, watching him as he stuffed the newspaper inside a rubbish sack propped up behind one of the other caravans. As soon as he was out of sight Lexi rushed over to rescue the paper. It had been pushed well down under a pile of kitchen scraps and Lexi shook off some soggy potato peelings before bringing it over to Ava.

'This must be the paper Aunt Val was

 54

talking about,' Lexi said, studying the front page. 'I don't understand. We've been travelling around the south of England so far this summer. What's my uncle doing with a newspaper from so far away?'

The paper was a week old and as they flicked through it a particular photograph jumped out at them together with the headline BABY ELEPHANT STOLEN FROM ZOO.

Ava had butterflies in her tummy as Lexi read the article out loud. It gave details about the zoo and described how its star attraction – an

eight-month-old baby elephant called Bonnie – had been stolen from the elephant house in the middle of the night. '*Fancy's Zoo and Elephant Sanctuary purchased Bonnie along with her mother, Grace, six months ago, stating that they wanted to give them a home where they could stay together,*' Lexi read slowly. '*The zoo, which opened only last year, has received much praise for the excellent care and living conditions it provides for its elephants. The zoo's owner, Mister Hugh Fancy, is extremely distressed by the loss of baby Bonnie and is eager to hear from anyone with any information. Bonnie apparently has one distinguishing mark – a V-shaped scar on her left ear.*'

The two girls looked at one another.

'Come on,' said Lexi finally. 'Let's go and find out.'

★

 56

They found Sukey standing with her back
to them inside the lorry. She looked round
when she heard Lexi's voice and took a few
steps towards them. Lexi spoke to her softly
and pulled an apple out from her pocket,
which Sukey spotted at once. As Lexi fed
it to her she told Ava, 'It took me ages to
get her to trust me. I've spent hours just
sitting here stroking her and talking to her
and feeding her apples. I think she's finally
realized I'm her friend.'

Just as Lexi was about to take a closer look
at Sukey's left ear they heard a gruff, all-too-
familiar voice. It was Max.

'What are you two doing in here again?'
he barked. 'Lexi, I thought I told you I
don't want you fussing over that animal!
She's not a pet. She's got to earn her keep.'

'Sorry, Uncle Max,' Lexi said quickly.

'I've still got to feed her and muck her out though, haven't I? Unless you want Gemma or Dulcie to do it?'

He scowled. 'Of course not! That's still your job until Tommy starts tomorrow.' He paused. 'Yes . . . well . . . you'd better get on with it then!'

'I can help too if you like,' Ava offered.

'What – in *that* outfit?' Max said, laughing. 'Watch out then! You don't want to lose that tiara in a pile of elephant dung!'

'It's OK, Ava.' Lexi looked like she was trying not to laugh too. 'Why don't you go and see how Marietta's getting on and I'll come and find you when I'm finished.'

6

Marietta was in the big top clipping on her red trousers, chatting to Tony as he pulled on a pair of jeans over his shorts.

As Ava entered the tent she passed Gemma and Dulcie, who were watching Marietta and Tony from the side.

'Hey, Ava!' Gemma said, putting out her hand to grab Ava. 'I told you to warn your aunt to back off. This is *our* act, not hers.'

'Yes – and she's too clumsy to be a trapeze artist in any case,' Dulcie added cattily.

'What do you mean? Marietta *isn't*

clumsy!' Ava protested, trying in vain to pull her arm away from Gemma's grip.

'She swings badly,' Dulcie said. 'And that means she's awkward to catch. I just hope Tony doesn't sprain his wrists trying to catch her.'

'He might even drop her,' Gemma said. 'I hope she knows how to fall. Clumsy people often fall very badly, I've noticed . . .'

'Ava, over here!' Marietta called out to her, and Ava broke away from Gemma and hurried across to join her aunt, who was smiling happily. 'Ava – say hello to Tony!'

'So this is the niece I've heard so much about,' Tony greeted Ava, grinning broadly. He was tanned and very muscular – especially his arms, which Ava guessed had to be strong to support him on the trapeze.

'Hi, Tony,' Ava said shyly.

'So, how do you like our circus then, Ava?' he asked her.

'Oh, very much!' she gushed.

'Good! Has Marietta told you I've finally managed to persuade her to star in my act tonight?'

'*Tonight?*' Ava was shocked. 'Is she good enough already then?'

Marietta laughed. 'That was *my* point, Ava!'

'There's nothing for you to worry about, Ava,' Tony teased. 'If she makes a complete fool of herself you can always pretend you don't know her, OK?'

'No, it's not that,' Ava said as Marietta gave Tony a playful thump. Ava wanted to talk to Marietta about the twins, but she wasn't sure if she ought to while Tony was there. 'I'm wondering if it's completely *safe*, that's all,' she continued. 'I mean, what if she falls?'

'Then she'll fall into the net, won't she?' Tony said lightly.

'Yes, but won't it *hurt*?' Ava asked, glancing up at the large rope net distrustfully.

'Not if you know how to bounce. It's a bit like landing on a big trampoline.'

'A trampoline? Really?' Ava had recently taken trampoline classes at her local sports centre. It had been really good fun and she had learned lots of great moves. In fact she had been wondering if she would be allowed to try out the circus trampoline while she was here.

Seeing her glancing over at it, Tony asked, 'Would you like a go while there's nobody else on it?'

 62

'Oh, yes please!' she exclaimed.

Ava was soon having such a wonderful time that she decided to stay on the trampoline while Marietta and Tony went off to Tony's caravan to get some lunch. They hadn't been gone long when she looked up to see Lexi cartwheeling across the ring towards her.

'Wow!' Ava exclaimed in admiration.

'Wow yourself!' Lexi said when she reached her. 'You're really good on that thing. We'll make an acrobat out of you yet, I reckon!'

Ava laughed as she jumped down from the trampoline and picked up the butterfly wings and her tiara, which she had taken off while she was bouncing. She lowered her voice as she asked Lexi, 'So? Did you see it?'

63

Lexi nodded. 'A V-shaped scar just like the paper said. Come on! Let's go and find Stella!'

As Ava placed the tiara back on her head Lexi let out a sudden gasp. 'Wow! How did you make it do that?'

'Do what?' Ava asked in surprise.

'Just now . . . when you put your tiara on . . . it sort of . . . well . . . *lit up!*'

'Oh!' Ava frowned, because she had forgotten about the tiara reacting whenever a person with the travelling gift put it on.

Lexi was still looking at her for an explanation.

'It must have been a trick of the light,' Ava muttered, and she flushed bright red because she had never been very good at lying.

★

Stella was frowning as she read the
newspaper article about the missing baby
elephant. They were inside her caravan,
seated in the small dining booth with
the blue leather seats and cheerful spotty

cushions. A white wooden screen with a
bright yellow abstract flower design on it
had been placed between the living space

and the sleeping area where the magic mirror was situated.

'You *do* believe us now, don't you?' Lexi said urgently as Stella looked up. 'The scar is definitely there because I've just been to check.'

Stella nodded grimly. 'Max is not only completely heartless but he's a total fool. Your grandfather gave your dad overall control of the circus when he retired because he didn't trust Max, and now I can see why!' She shook her head in disbelief. 'Max must think this zoo is so far away from here that no one will put two and two together. Goodness knows how he arranged it.'

'Now we *know* Sukey's stolen, can't we just call the police and tell them she's here?' Ava suggested. 'We can do it anonymously

so no one will know it was us.'

'We can't involve the police,' Stella said
at once. 'It would cause too much trouble
for the circus. No . . . we'll take her back to
the zoo ourselves. I've driven circus lorries
plenty of times before. Let's have a look
at the map.' She got out a large dog-eared
road atlas and started to search through it.
'OK,' she murmured when she eventually
found the small town where the zoo was
located. 'It's a long way, but I should be
able to easily get there and back in time
for tomorrow's show. The two of you will
need to come with me and help with Sukey
though.'

'You mean Bonnie,' Lexi corrected her
quietly. 'That's her real name so we have to
start calling her that now.'

Their conversation was interrupted by

a sharp rap at the door.

It was Val. 'Ah, Lexi . . .' she said, stepping inside uninvited as Stella quickly shoved the newspaper under the table. 'Tony said you might be here. I'm off to the village to place a call to your mother. Do you want to come?'

'Oh, yes please, Aunt Val,' Lexi said, jumping up.

Val was looking at Ava curiously. 'So you're Marietta's niece, are you?' Her gaze shifted rapidly from Ava's face to her tiara, where it stayed for what seemed like forever. Ava felt very uncomfortable.

As soon as they'd gone Stella turned to Ava and said, 'Luckily my act is one of the first in the show, so as soon as I'm finished we can drive off with Bonnie in the lorry. Hopefully everyone else will be too busy with the show to notice we've gone. We'll leave a note for Marietta in my caravan so she doesn't get too worried about you.'

Ava frowned. 'Stella, what do you think Max will do when he finds out?'

'Oh, he'll fire *me* for sure, but then I wouldn't want to keep working here with him as the boss anyway.'

'And what about Lexi?'

'Max will be angry, but he won't hurt her. Don't worry about that.' She paused. 'I just hope we're doing the right thing. I mean zoos don't exactly make the most wonderful homes for elephants either, do they?'

Ava thought about how her mum had never liked zoos, disapproving of wild animals being kept in captivity. But Ava also knew that zoos did a lot of valuable conservation work – at least, they did in the time *she* lived in . . .

'This sounds like a pretty *good* zoo,' she pointed out. 'And besides, I'm sure Sukey – Bonnie, I mean – would rather be in a zoo with her mum than all alone in a circus where she hasn't even got any other elephants to keep her company.'

'That's true of course,' Stella agreed, sounding more determined as she added, 'Anyway, I'm sure it's what Lexi's dad would want us to do and as far as I'm concerned *he's* still the boss, not Max!' She stood up. 'Right then, I'm getting hungry. Shall I make us both a sandwich?'

'Oh, yes please!' Ava said gratefully, for she was starting to regret missing lunch.

'Potted beef or fish paste?' Stella offered

cheerfully as she reached up into a small food cupboard.

'Er . . .' Ava did her best not to pull a face, but it was difficult to hide her relief when Stella remembered that she had a pot of strawberry jam as well.

7

Ava had never been to a circus performance of any kind before and she felt excited along with the rest of the audience as she sat in her seat that evening waiting for the show to begin. The atmosphere was a bit like the kind you got at a Christmas pantomime, Ava thought.

Lexi had found her an unsold seat near the front and as she handed her a carton of popcorn she told Ava she would see her at the lorry.

'Aren't you going to stay and watch the show?' Ava asked her.

 72

Lexi shook her head. 'The only bit I haven't seen a million times before is Marietta on the trapeze and we'll have to leave before that in any case.'

At the mention of Marietta Ava felt her stomach start to churn and as she watched Lexi slip out through the nearest exit she found that she couldn't eat her popcorn. If only she had managed to talk to Marietta about Gemma and Dulcie – but she hadn't even seen her aunt since lunchtime.

The band were seated in a balcony over the performers' entrance and it was the conductor who signalled the start of the show by raising his baton for the music to begin. A massive spotlight immediately shone down on to the ring as the ringmaster emerged through the performers' entrance to greet the audience.

73

'LADIES AND GENTLEMEN, BOYS AND GIRLS . . .' he called out grandly through his handheld megaphone, 'WITHOUT FURTHER ADO . . . LET THE SHOW BEGIN!'

Everything happened in quick succession after that. The first act was a troupe of acrobats – a mass of colour in their bright, shiny costumes. Next came a sword-swallower – whose performance Ava could hardly bear to watch. Some light relief was provided by a very funny, hat-juggling clown. Then it was Stella's turn.

Stella looked amazing as she entered the ring in a pink-and-gold-sequinned catsuit. First she did a floor display showing off a selection of incredible poses involving back-bends, front-bends and leg-splits. Then she folded herself up inside a small leather suitcase and was wheeled around the ring on a porter's luggage trolley before bursting free from the case in one dramatic leap. The audience loved it and the clapping and cheering seemed like it would never stop.

For her finale Stella took up the same position Ava had seen her rehearse outside, balanced on her hands on top of a T-shaped pole in the middle of the ring. It was hard to believe that her body was made of anything other than rubber as she performed the amazing back-bend, this time with a wooden crossbow gripped between her feet, which she aimed at a target on the other side of the ring.

'LADIES AND GENTLEMEN,' came the ringmaster's playful voice, 'PRINCESS STELLA HAS NEVER YET HIT A MEMBER OF OUR AUDIENCE, BUT OF COURSE THERE IS ALWAYS A FIRST TIME . . .' As the audience laughed, he made a request for complete silence so as not to 'tempt fate', as he put it.

'HURRAH!' came the massive cheer from the crowd as Stella hit the target right in the middle – and Ava cheered louder than anyone.

As Stella left the stage amidst thunderous applause Ava knew it was time for her to go too. She quickly slipped out of her seat and started to make for the same exit Lexi had taken earlier.

76

But just before she reached it a sharp voice called out her name and she turned to see Gemma wearing a silky silver robe. She was clutching a large leather drawstring pouch and she looked unusually anxious.

As Ava looked past Gemma she felt her stomach flip over as she saw Marietta prancing into the ring arm in arm with Tony. They both looked very regal in their long shiny trapeze capes, and Marietta's red hair was glittering magically under the spotlight, almost as if it had been sprinkled with tiny diamonds before being fastened into its bun. Marietta ripped off her silk trousers with a flourish at the foot of the ladder and Tony turned her round to wave to the audience before an assistant came to relieve them of their capes. Then as the orchestra struck up the music for their act

Marietta began
to climb the
rope ladder
to the fliers'
platform while
Tony shimmied
up a rope to
the catcher's
swing.

'LADIES
AND GENTLEMEN, BOYS AND
GIRLS,' the ringmaster was announcing.
'IN ADDITION TO OUR VERY
OWN HIGH-FLYING ACROBATS
TONY AND THE TRAPEZE TWINS,
WE HAVE A SURPRISE IN OUR
PROGRAMME . . . OVERCOMING
HER FEAR OF HEIGHTS IN THIS,
HER DEBUT PERFORMANCE,

LADIES AND GENTLEMEN . . . MAY
I PRESENT . . . THE BEAUTIFUL . . .
THE BRAVE . . . *MISS MARIETTA*!'

'Marietta hasn't *got* a fear of heights,' Ava
murmured, frowning.

'Of course not, but the audience
don't know that, do they?' Gemma said
impatiently. 'Listen, Ava, we have to get this
to Marietta as quickly as possible.'

'What is it?' Ava asked, looking
suspiciously at the drawstring pouch Gemma
was holding out.

'Chalk. When you're on the trapeze your
hands get sweaty and you need this to absorb
the moisture. Otherwise your hands get so
slippy you can lose your grip on the bar.
Marietta's forgotten to take it with her.'

'Oh no . . .' Ava frowned because that
didn't sound good.

'I'd take it up to her myself, but I've still got to finish getting changed and by then it might be too late. That's why *you'll* have to do it, Ava.'

'Me?' Ava felt her stomach starting to churn. 'But . . . but can't Dulcie—'

'I can't *find* Dulcie.' Gemma cut her off briskly. 'Come on . . . We'll have to be quick . . .' She led Ava out of the big top, round the outside a short way and in again through a back entrance. There Ava found herself in a changing area amidst a bustle of performers getting themselves ready. Gemma took hold of Ava's arm and led her through the performers' entrance into the ring. The circus spotlight was trained upward to illuminate the trapeze act, leaving the ring in relative darkness.

'Come on, Ava,' Gemma instructed,

leading her over to the bottom of the rope ladder, where she unhooked Ava's butterfly wings.

Ava gulped. She had climbed rope ladders before in the gym at school, though never one as high as this. Nervously she put one foot on the first rung.

Nobody in the audience seemed to notice that anything out of the ordinary was happening as Ava pulled herself up on to the next rung – and the next. She guessed they must just assume she was part of the act. Maybe it was the adrenaline or maybe it was the magic in her trapeze costume – but she hardly felt any fear as she climbed upwards.

As she swung herself up on to the trapeze platform – which was little more than a broad plank of wood suspended by some cables from the roof – she was taken aback to find Dulcie elegantly poised at one end of it, wearing a sparkly silver trapeze costume.

'Oh, look!' Dulcie sneered. 'If it isn't *Little Miss Butterfly* . . . You'd better be careful. It's quite dangerous up here without your wings, you know!'

Ava said nothing, aware of her pulse thumping loudly inside her ears. She watched Marietta do an impressive flip off the trapeze swing to be caught in mid-air by Tony. The crowd clapped and then clapped again as Marietta did a simple but neat twist back to the empty bar.

'*Ava!*' Marietta exclaimed, getting a huge shock as she swung back to the platform and found her there. She nearly lost her balance as Dulcie snatched the bar very roughly from her hands and swung off expertly towards Tony.

 82

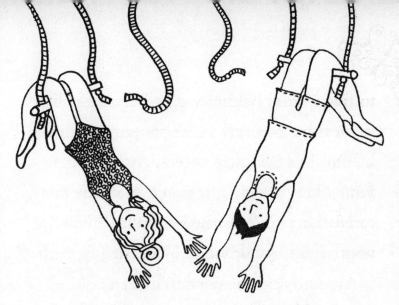

'I came to give you this,' Ava told
Marietta breathlessly, holding out the bag of
chalk. 'Gemma said you need it to stop you
slipping off the bar.'

'What are you talking about?' Marietta
looked puzzled as she pointed to a much
larger drawstring leather bag attached to one
of the side ropes. It was open at the top and
full of a white powder, which Ava realized
was also chalk.

'I don't understand,' Ava mumbled.

Just then Gemma climbed up on to the

platform from below. She had discarded her silver robe to reveal a silver trapeze costume identical to her sister's. 'Yes, Ava, what *are* you talking about?' she sneered. She turned to Marietta. 'We warned you that things might get nasty up here if you tried to push in on our act. You wouldn't listen before, but now Ava's here maybe you will!'

Ava stared from Gemma to Marietta, still not understanding.

'Ava, I think we'd better both climb back down right now,' Marietta said, sounding very wary all of a sudden. 'Come on. I'll help you.'

Ava nodded, satisfied that at least Marietta was coming off the trapeze with her, but when she looked down at the ladder it was as if a giant dose of reality suddenly met her head-on. All at once she felt dizzy, her

legs felt wobbly and she was certain she
was going to fall. 'I don't . . . think . . . I
can . . .' she stammered, and suddenly all
she could think about was holding on for
dear life as the big top seemed to be rotating
around her.

'Ava, sit down
and take some
deep breaths,'
Marietta
instructed her,
sounding tense.
'I'll help you . . .
that's it . . . it's just
like sitting on a swing . . . now, sit there and
hold on tight . . . it's going to be all right.'

But Marietta had reckoned without
Dulcie, who was swinging back towards
them, hanging upside down by her knees.

85

Quick as lightning Dulcie reached out and grabbed Ava's dangling ankles. '*Gotcha!*'

Ava let out a scream as she was yanked right off the platform and swung through the air upside down, her tiara falling off her head and hurtling to the ground amidst lots of oohs and aahs from the audience.

'Smile, Little Miss Butterfly – you're the star of the show!' Dulcie shouted cheerily. And she swung Ava to and fro a few more times, before calling out in a mischievous voice, 'Oops . . . Butterfingers!' as she let go.

8

Ava screamed the whole way down, hitting the net with a thud that knocked her breath away before shooting back up again. She curled herself up again instinctively for the next bounce, terrified the whole time that she was going to bounce right out of the net.

Val was the first to reach her, shouting

up to ask if she was OK. The trapeze act seemed to be continuing above them as the ringmaster made an announcement to reassure the audience. Ava wasn't listening to what he said. All she could hear was her own rapid breathing as her heart thumped away manically inside her chest. With Val's help she managed to swing down over the side of the net, trembling and close to tears as she landed on the ground.

Val was dressed in a bright red corset-and-feathers outfit, with a feather boa and a matching silky cape. She immediately sat Ava down and went off to get her a drink of water, returning after a few minutes with a grubby looking glass. 'What a carry-on up there! I don't know!' She shook her head disapprovingly as she watched Ava take a sip.

'Wait till I get hold of those two!'

Marietta snapped as she joined them, having just climbed as fast as she could down the rope ladder. 'Ava's never been on a trapeze before! She could have been killed!' Her cheeks were flushed as she handed Ava her butterfly wings. 'As for you, miss,' she told her crossly. 'I'm taking you straight home!'

'But Gemma said—'

'No buts!' Marietta interrupted her. 'I don't care *what* Gemma told you – you should never have climbed up there! Now I know how your dad felt, when he had to look after *me* as a kid and I was always running off and doing something stupid!'

Ava had never seen Marietta lose her cool before. She didn't know what to say, but she did know that there was no way she was ready to go home yet. She remembered that she was meant to have joined Stella and Lexi at the lorry by now and she only hoped they hadn't already left without her.

'Wait!' Ava protested, pulling her arm away as Marietta helped her up. 'I have to . . . to say goodbye to Lexi first . . . and . . . and . . . what about my tiara? I *can't* go home without that.'

Marietta seemed to calm down a little. 'OK – you go and see Lexi. I'll come and find you after I've spoken to Tony. We'll have to wait until the interval in any case, to look for your tiara. It's got to be in the ring somewhere, or maybe it's caught in the net.'

Just then Val let out a scream as she spotted a big spider running over the ground near her foot. As she jumped sideways, she bumped into Ava, and something fell out from under her cape. It was Ava's tiara.

As Ava picked it up from the floor, Val went bright red and started to mumble something about being about to give it to them when the spider had distracted her.

Marietta was looking furious and Ava would have liked to stay and hear what she had to say to Val. But there was no time – not if she wanted to catch up with the others.

The lorry was gone when Ava got there and she felt so disappointed she almost started to cry. Then she glanced across the field to the gate and saw the lorry parked in the lane just outside.

'Where have you been?' Stella hissed, leaning out of the driver's window as Ava approached. The lorry's engine was ticking over and she was clearly keen to get going.

91

'Never mind. Tell us when you get your breath back.'

'Goodness, why haven't you changed into some normal clothes?' Lexi asked as Ava climbed up into the cab, slamming the door shut behind her.

'I was in a rush,' Ava murmured, reaching up to check her tiara was on securely, relieved that she had decided to leave her wings behind. She felt a bit guilty about running out on Marietta like this, but at least Stella had left her a note in her caravan explaining where they'd gone.

Stella released the lorry's handbrake, keeping the headlights switched off so as not to attract attention. Ava had never ridden in the cab of a lorry before and she was surprised by how high up off the ground it seemed compared to being a passenger in a car.

'How long do you think it'll take us to get there?' Ava asked as soon as they were out of sight of the circus encampment.

'If all goes well about five or six hours, I should think,' Stella said. 'You girls should try and get some sleep.'

'Oh, I couldn't *sleep*!' Ava protested.

'Me neither!' agreed Lexi.

Stella laughed. 'Well, we'll see . . .'

'Will Sukey . . . I mean Bonnie . . . be all right shut up in the back the whole way?' Ava asked.

'She's got lots of water to drink and plenty of fruit and veggies to eat, and I wedged open the back door a little at the top to let in some air,' Stella replied. 'She should be fine, but you can check on her if you pull

93

back that little curtain just above your head.'

Ava twisted round in her seat to find a small dusty curtain covering a window that allowed those in the driver's cab to see into the back of the lorry.

Ava could see Bonnie sucking up some water into her trunk from a metal bucket that was tethered to the floor. 'She's having a drink,' Ava reported. But instead of squirting the water into her mouth, Bonnie lifted up her trunk and sprayed the water all over her back. 'Oh, wait . . . she's giving herself a bath instead!'

Lexi knelt up against the back of her seat to look too. 'Hey, Bonnie – are you trying to get rid of all those nasty circus smells before you go back to your mother?' she joked.

And Bonnie raised her head and gave a loud snort as if she agreed.

 94

'Ava, wake up!' It was dark outside and
Stella was shaking her gently.

For a few moments Ava couldn't think
where she was as she sat up sleepily, rubbing
her eyes. She reached up to check her tiara
was still on her head as she asked, 'What's
happened? Is something wrong?'

'We're here,' Stella said softly. 'It's two
o'clock in the morning. You've both been
asleep for the last four hours.'

Beside her, Ava saw that Lexi was just
stirring too.

'Look. That's the entrance to the zoo,'
Stella said. They had arrived at the end of a
quiet road and the lorry was parked in front
of a pair of big iron gates locked together
with a metal chain. Fixed to the wall on
one side of the gates, and illuminated by

a lamp directly above it, was a sign that
read: FANCY'S ZOO AND ELEPHANT
SANCTUARY.

'Listen, I've been thinking,' Stella
continued. 'I reckon we should tie
Bonnie up to the gates and call the police
anonymously to tell them she's here. We
passed a phone box further back along the
road. You girls can stay here with Bonnie
and I'll drive back and make the call. Then
I'll park the lorry somewhere where it won't
be noticed and come back here on foot.
When the police get here we can hide and
watch what happens.'

Bonnie seemed to approve of their plan,
for she trotted readily out of the lorry when
Stella put down the ramp for her.

But as the lorry reversed down the
road away from them Ava started to feel

uneasy. The full moon, which had been shining brightly when they had arrived, had disappeared behind a cloud, and without the lorry's headlights they were in darkness apart from the dim circle of light coming from the lamp outside the zoo entrance. Lexi didn't seem to be aware of anything other than Bonnie as she stood with her arms around the elephant, whispering goodbye as Bonnie made little snorty sounds and curled her trunk affectionately around Lexi's neck.

Ava waited tensely, jumping at every sound until, after what seemed forever, the moon came out again and they could see better. Shortly afterwards a pair of headlights appeared along the road.

'Quick, Lexi! We'd better hide!' Ava exclaimed in alarm, but then she saw that it was their own lorry returning.

'Don't worry, Bonnie. It's only Stella . . .' Lexi murmured.

'I thought Stella said she was going to *walk* back,' Ava said, wondering why the plan had suddenly changed.

They soon found out after the lorry came to a halt right in front of them, its headlamps shining directly on to Bonnie and the two girls. As Ava and Lexi shielded their eyes from the glare the headlamps were switched off abruptly.

'Did you really think I wouldn't find you?' came a gruff male voice as the driver's door was flung open and a bulky figure jumped down from the cab.

'*Uncle Max!*' Lexi gasped in horror, quickly going to stand beside Bonnie. 'How did *you* get here?'

9

'Where's Stella?' Ava demanded as her eyes gradually adjusted to the moonlight again.

'In there,' Max replied, pointing to the back of the lorry, from where they could now make out a muffled yelling. The corners of his mouth twitched slightly as he added, 'Tied up with Val's feather boa!'

As he spoke a small van had driven up behind the lorry and now its occupant stepped out.

'Aunt Val!' Lexi exclaimed.

Ava watched, too scared to move, half expecting Val to produce two more feather boas to tie up herself and Lexi.

Instead Val ignored Ava and narrowed her eyes at her niece, snapping, '*You* need a lesson in family loyalty, young lady. It's lucky we caught Stella before she'd had time to phone anybody!' She marched Lexi over to the van and told her to sit in the front passenger seat and keep quiet. 'Otherwise you won't be spending any time at all with that elephant after we get her back to the circus,' she added before slamming the door shut and locking it.

Val came back to address Ava, pausing as if momentarily distracted by her tiara before asking, 'Right . . . are *you* going to start causing trouble now?'

Ava shook her head, unable to speak.

'Good. Well, just you wait there and keep quiet. It's thanks to your auntie that we're here, by the way. I've never seen anyone get into such a panic about a missing kid! If she hadn't raised the alarm so quickly we wouldn't have realized in time that the lorry was gone.'

'But we left Marietta a note,' Ava mumbled, puzzled.

Val smiled. 'Yes, but she didn't find it straight away. It had fallen on the floor or something. After she read it she calmed down, but by then Max and I had guessed what was going on.'

'Oh,' Ava murmured, feeling even more miserable.

Meanwhile Bonnie had started to make a high-pitched squealing sound as Max approached her with a loop of rope. Bonnie clearly sensed what he was trying to do as she kept moving her head, swishing her trunk angrily and doing her best to ram into him when he came too close. When he tried speaking to her in a sickeningly coaxing voice, she didn't fall for it, swiping out at him and letting out more loud squeals as she butted him with her huge frame, almost knocking him off his feet.

And then, from inside the zoo, they heard another sound – a distant trumpeting.

'I bet that's her mother,' Ava gasped.

Bonnie obviously heard it

too for she immediately turned towards the noise and responded with a similar call.

Quick as lightning Max darted forward and threw the rope around Bonnie's neck. Then as Bonnie continued to concentrate on letting her mother know that she was there Max untied her from the gate. He tried to tug her towards the lorry but Bonnie stubbornly refused to go, squealing even more loudly for her mother to come and rescue her. Finally Max told Val to go to the van and fetch the pitchfork they had brought with them.

'Wait! Don't hurt her,' Ava begged, starting to cry. As Val returned with the pitchfork, Ava rushed forward to stop Max using it, but Val grabbed her and held on to her tightly.

'MOVE!' Max barked at Bonnie, raising

the pitchfork ready to thrust it into her side.

Ava knew she had to do something – but what?

'If you let Bonnie go you can have my tiara!' she shouted desperately. Val dug her fingernails hard into Ava's arm. 'What did you say?'

'I'm saying that if you let her go then you can have the tiara and I promise I won't tell anyone you've got it! It's made of rubies *and* amethysts *and* orange diamonds, so it should be worth lots of money!'

Max lowered the pitchfork and stared at Ava. 'Did you say orange *diamonds*?'

'That's right. I think they must be very rare . . .' Her mouth had gone dry and her own voice sounded strange.

'I *told* you the jewels on that thing were real, Max,' Val hissed, letting go of Ava's arm, 'but you wouldn't have it.'

Max still didn't seem totally convinced. 'That's because it doesn't make any sense. I mean, what circus trapeze girl would own a thing like that?'

'Oh, I haven't always been a trapeze girl,' Ava said quickly. 'My family . . . you see . . . my family have many beautiful tiaras . . .'

'I knew it!' Val exclaimed. 'Neither her nor her aunt are circus folk! I could tell straight away there was something different about them. Marietta has always pretended she's from circus stock but it's not true. The two of them are rich-kid runaways – that's what they are. I bet that tiara's worth a fortune!'

Max frowned at Ava. 'But if we do give back the elephant, how do we know you'll keep your word?'

'I promise I will,' Ava said. 'And I won't tell *anyone* you've got the tiara – not even Marietta. I'll just say that I lost it.'

'Max, let's do it!' Val said, her eyes gleaming as she stared greedily at the tiara. 'We're talking about giving up an annoying little elephant who, from what I've seen, has turned out to be far more trouble than she's worth. Think about it, Max. With the money from those jewels we could set up our *own* circus. Then you can have all the performing animals you want!'

Ava felt a bit sick, realizing that with the money from her tiara they could purchase many more baby elephants like Bonnie. But she didn't have time to think about it because the lorry's back door suddenly burst open and something large and cat-like leaped out and came bounding towards them.

'Stella!' Ava exclaimed as the figure pounced right on top of Max. Ignoring his cries, Stella sat on his shoulders while she pummelled him repeatedly with her fists.

'I don't . . . understand! How did . . . you get . . . free?' Max spluttered as he squirmed about, trying in vain to shake her off.

'I'm a contortionist and escapologist, you idiot!' Stella yelled. 'Did you really think I'd be thwarted by *this*?' And she stuck her hand in her pocket and pulled out a handful of bright red feathers.

'My feather boa!' Val exclaimed furiously.

'More feathers than boa now, Val!' Stella snapped as she tossed the handful up into the air.

And as the feathers showered down over a horrified Val, Ava found it difficult not to laugh.

10

Ava hadn't realized just how strongly Stella felt about not causing any trouble for the circus.

Instead of making Max and Val stay and face the police, Stella let them drive off in their van – but only after they had promised to be gone from the circus by the end of the weekend.

Stella was just opening the driver's door of the lorry, ready to go and make her anonymous phone call about Bonnie when they saw another vehicle approaching. It was difficult to see properly in the moonlight

but it looked like an ordinary car with two people in the front.

Stella immediately got the girls back inside the cab of the lorry before going to stand protectively beside Bonnie. Ava held her breath as the car came to a standstill alongside them, its engine still running. What would the occupants say when they saw Bonnie? What would Stella say to explain why they were there?

Ava had her nose pressed against the lorry's side window watching the car. She let out a gasp as the driver's door opened and a circus clown stepped out. As he crossed in front of the car he was fully illuminated by its headlights and Ava saw that he wore orange baggy trousers, a green coat with enormous red spots, and a silly hat with a fake flower growing out of the side. His painted clown's face made him unrecognizable even in the lamplight, although there was something about him that seemed vaguely familiar.

The clown went over to speak to Stella and after a few minutes Stella pointed at the lorry.

'I don't understand . . .' Lexi murmured as the clown started to walk towards them.

Ava did though, and now she was opening her door. 'Dad!' she burst out, jumping down from the cab to greet him. As they hugged each other she gasped, 'I didn't recognize you at first, dressed like that!'

'I know. I asked Marietta for a costume that would help me blend in and this is what she produced . . . Still, I suppose I'm lucky not to be wearing a sparkly leotard.

Now . . . are you all right?'

'Oh, yes . . . and I'm sorry I left the circus without telling anybody, but Marietta was going to make me go home, and I *really* wanted to help bring Bonnie back to the zoo.'

'That's no excuse, Ava,' her dad said sternly. 'And don't think we won't be talking more about this later. But right now I need to take a closer look at Bonnie.'

Ava was puzzled. 'Why, Dad?'

But he didn't answer her, and as he went back over to join Stella and Bonnie, who was starting to get restless, Ava suddenly saw that Marietta was getting out of the car.

'Hello, Ava,' her aunt greeted her coldly.

'Sorry, Marietta,' Ava said at once.

'So you should be. And, Stella . . . I thought we were friends!'

Stella looked guilty as she walked towards Marietta. 'Sorry. I thought if I left you a note stuck to the mirror then you'd understand and wouldn't worry . . .'

'Yes, well you couldn't have stuck it on very well . . . it was on the floor and I'd done plenty of worrying by the time I found it!'

'Marietta, please don't be cross with Stella,' Ava begged, feeling terrible.

'Yes,' Lexi chipped in. 'She was just helping us get Bonnie back to her mum.'

'Speaking of which,' Stella said swiftly, 'I really ought to go and phone the police.'

'Why don't you leave that to us?' Dad suggested, quickly looking up from his inspection of Bonnie.

'Really? Well . . . if you're sure . . .' Stella sounded relieved. 'I'd certainly like to get Lexi back to the circus as quickly as possible. I can take Ava back too if you want.'

'That's OK,' Ava's dad replied. 'Ava can come back with us.' He looked at his sister. 'Marietta, how about you go and make that call now, while Ava and I stay here with Bonnie?'

Ava stood with her arms around Bonnie as they watched Stella and Lexi leave in the lorry. Marietta had already driven off ahead of them in the car.

'It won't be long now, Bonnie,' Ava murmured, gently stroking the baby elephant on the front of her trunk.

As Dad came to stand in front of Bonnie again, the elephant greeted him with soft, trusting eyes. 'Ava, lend me your tiara for a moment, will you?' he said.

'Why?' Ava asked in surprise as she handed it over.

'Watch.' Her dad carefully placed the tiara on Bonnie's head. Not only did Bonnie look extremely cute wearing it, but the tiara seemed to glow extra brightly all of a sudden.

'She has the travelling gift,' Dad said at once. As Ava stared at Bonnie in disbelief he added, 'It's not just humans who have it, you know. Remember Cindy . . .'

Ava was stunned. It was true that Ava's pet cat, Cindy, had proved that *cats* could have the gift when she had travelled through a magic mirror to Cinderella-land. But Ava hadn't thought before about other animals having it too.

'So is *that* why Bonnie seems so relaxed with us?' Ava eventually asked slowly. 'Because she senses we have the same gift as her?'

'Probably, though I think she also just senses that we're on her side. Elephants are very intelligent, sensitive creatures – and not just the travelling ones.'

As he spoke, Bonnie reached up with her trunk and removed the tiara from her head, offering it back to Ava with a friendly grunt.

'Thank you, Bonnie!' Ava said with a giggle.

Her dad smiled and waited for Ava to put the tiara back on her own head before suddenly looking more serious. 'Ava, I know how badly you want to reunite Bonnie with her mother, but I'd like to speak to the zoo's owner first. I want to make sure we're not moving her out of the frying pan into the fire so to speak.'

'What do you mean?' Ava asked in surprise.

'Here.' Dad pulled a folded sheet of newspaper and a pen-torch out of his pocket. 'When Marietta came to tell me you had gone off with Stella to take an elephant

 116

back to Fancy's Zoo, I remembered an article I'd read in the newspaper a couple of weeks ago. Luckily I still had it. Look.' He shone his torch on the torn-out page so that Ava could read it.

DISAPPEARING ZOO OWNER TAKES SECRET TO THE GRAVE, the headline read. *Mr Hugh Fancy, owner of the ill-fated Fancy's Zoo and Elephant Sanctuary, has died at the age of 97. In the 1950s Fancy's elephant sanctuary became famous after Mr Fancy and his entire collection of Indian elephants mysteriously vanished in the middle of the night. A full investigation took place at the time, including a detailed search of the zoo's grounds, but the fate of Mr Fancy and his elephants was to become one of the biggest unsolved mysteries of the decade . . .* Ava stopped reading and stared at her dad. 'It's the nineteen fifties *now*, isn't it?'

He nodded. 'Keep going. You can skip the next part with all the dates and details. Just read the paragraph at the end.'

. . . One winter's morning, thirty years later, Mr Fancy reappeared in a hospital A & E department, apparently suffering from a total loss of memory. Sadly, throughout the rest of his long life he was unable to shed any light on the mystery of his missing elephants.

'I don't understand!' Ava exclaimed. 'What happened to all those elephants, and does this mean that if we leave Bonnie here then *she's* going to disappear too?'

'I've a pretty good idea what it means,' her dad replied, 'but I need to find out for sure. That's why I've asked Marietta not to phone the police but to see if she can find Mr Fancy in the local phone book instead.'

★

It didn't take long for Marietta to return
with the news that Mr Hugh Fancy lived in
a house within the zoo grounds and that he
was coming to meet them at the gates just as
soon as he was dressed. In fact she had barely
finished telling them this when they spotted
the flickering light of a torch
a short distance away on the
other side of the gates.

Mr Fancy turned
out to be a man
who looked about
the same age as
Ava's dad. He wore
round spectacles and had
untidy dark hair and Ava
thought he looked a bit
like an eccentric professor.
He unlocked the gates

and shrieked with delight when he saw
Bonnie – hugging her and kissing her and
thanking everyone repeatedly. Apparently
he suspected an ex-employee of organizing
the theft, and since the man had left the area
before the police could question him, the
zoo owner had almost given up hope of ever
seeing his baby elephant again.

If Mr Fancy thought it strange that
Bonnie's rescuers were all dressed in circus
costumes he didn't say so as he invited them
inside and led them up the lane, shining his
flashlight in front of them to show them the
way. Bonnie was only too happy to be led
along by Ava, clearly delighted to be home.

Dad and Mr Fancy walked slightly ahead
to start off with, talking quietly together.
Soon however they both turned around and
Dad announced, 'It's just as I thought. Mr

Fancy is a traveller like us and he has a magic
mirror right here in the zoo grounds.'

'These grounds and the mirror have been
in my family for generations,' Mr Fancy
explained. 'We have a small lake here and
the mirror lies under the water in a shallow
part, just at the edge. If a human – or an
animal – with the travelling gift looks
into the water at that spot they can be
transported through the portal to the other
side. But only if they're wearing an item
of magic clothing, of course, which is why
it doesn't happen to animals under normal
circumstances.'

'Tell them where your portal goes,' Dad
prompted him.

'It leads to a very beautiful stretch of land
in Northern India, which has been marked
out as a wildlife sanctuary. Hunting is

121

forbidden there and the elephants and other animals live together freely in the wild.'

'Wow!' Ava exclaimed.

'My plan is to gather together as many elephants with the travelling gift as I can from circuses and other zoos,' Mr Fancy continued. 'When I have enough I shall set them free to live as one herd on the

 122

other side of the magic portal. Of course, all the details will need to be worked out very carefully first . . . what item of magic clothing they could reasonably wear . . . how I shall explain their disappearance afterwards . . . whether *I* should disappear with them for a little while until all the fuss dies down . . .'

'Or for a *long* while . . .' Ava murmured, but her dad put his finger to his lips to warn her that they mustn't give away too much information about the future.

Ava stayed quiet after that, still curious about Mr Fancy's mysteriously long disappearance, but happy that everything else was falling into place. For not only were Bonnie and her mother about to be reunited, but soon they would be living freely in the wild.

11

The moon was out and shining brightly as
Mr Fancy showed Ava through a gate into
a massive grassy enclosure full of bushes and
trees. Opening on to it was the elephant
house, from where four adult elephants had
just emerged through a massive flap-like
door. One of them was making trumpeting
noises and pacing about in a very agitated
sort of way.

'Is that Bonnie's mother?' Ava whispered.

Mr Fancy nodded. 'Yes, that's Grace . . .
She's been beside herself since Bonnie was
taken. Now . . . you should be fine here.

Just stay well back and keep nice and quiet.'

Mr Fancy then went to fetch Bonnie, who was trumpeting excitedly as he released her into the enclosure through a larger gate a little further along from where he had positioned Ava.

Bonnie's mother immediately turned towards her baby and let out a piercing

cry of recognition. The two elephants
launched themselves at one other to
meet in the middle of the compound in
a kerfuffle of noise and obvious emotion.
In the moonlight Ava could see Bonnie's
mother touching her repeatedly with the
end of her trunk as Bonnie cuddled up to
her, full of shrieks and joyful snorts as her
world suddenly became a safe and familiar
place again. The other elephants came
trotting over to join in the welcome, and
Ava watched as Bonnie was gently nudged
underneath her mother's body, disappearing
from view behind a protective fence of
grown-up elephant legs.

Mr Fancy was smiling and rubbing tears
from his eyes as he came over to stand with
Ava. Ava was smiling too, grateful that
Bonnie's ordeal was finally over. But there

was still one thing she wanted to ask before
they rejoined the others.

'Mr Fancy, do you think you could be
happy if you had to stay on the other side of
your portal for a really long time? Actually
live *there* instead of *here*, I mean?'

He looked puzzled. 'Oh, yes . . . in some
ways I much prefer India to England. But
why do you want to know?'

'Oh, no reason,' Ava replied quickly.
But she couldn't help grinning and feeling
pleased that she had asked.

By the time Ava's dad had driven them
all the way back to the circus it was mid-
afternoon.

'I'll go and tell Tony we've brought back
his car,' Marietta said. 'I'll probably stay and
chat to him for a while, so don't wait for me.'

127

Ava and her dad headed for Stella's caravan and on the way they met Stella walking towards the big top with Lexi.

'Ava, this morning I got a telegram from my mum!' Lexi greeted her happily. 'My dad's going to be OK! He's finally started to respond to his treatment and the doctors say he should make a full recovery!'

'Oh, that's *wonderful*!' Ava burst out, giving Lexi a hug.

'Thank goodness,' Ava's dad said, smiling too.

'Mum says he's probably going to be moved out of intensive care tomorrow and then I can go and see him,' Lexi said. 'I can't wait to see Mum again as well!' Almost without pausing to breathe she continued, 'How did it go with Bonnie? I bet she was really happy to see *her*

 128

mum again too, wasn't she?'

Ava nodded, wishing she could tell her friend all about the zoo's magic mirror and Mr Fancy's future plans for Bonnie and the other elephants. Instead she described in detail the scene where the mother and baby had been reunited, while Lexi and Stella listened avidly.

'Are Max and Val still here?' Dad asked when Ava had finished.

'Yes, unfortunately,' Lexi said, pulling a face.

'But they're leaving tomorrow,' Stella added quickly. 'According to Val they're off to join another circus where they'll be better appreciated! Dulcie and Gemma didn't want to go with them at first, but they changed their minds after Tony told them he won't work with them on the trapeze any more.

He doesn't trust them after that stunt they pulled on Ava yesterday.'

'*What* stunt?' Dad asked at once, and Ava realized that Marietta couldn't have told him yet what had happened.

'They were trying to scare off Marietta and they decided to use Ava to do it,' Stella said.

'Use Ava *how*?' Dad demanded.

Fortunately his attention was temporarily diverted as Gemma and Dulcie came into view. For a moment Ava wondered if they were coming to apologize and she hoped they wouldn't say too much in front of her dad.

But of course she needn't have worried. As usual the twins were only thinking about themselves.

'Isn't it wonderful? Dulcie and I are to be

the stars in our family's new act!' Gemma boasted. 'Dad says we're going to bring the act some much-needed glamour.'

'Yes, and our new career in the *Impalement Arts* will be far more exciting than swinging about on that boring old trapeze with Tony,' Dulcie added haughtily.

Lexi was grinning. 'The Impalement Arts? Isn't that just a fancy way of saying *knife-throwing?*'

'Certainly not!' Dulcie responded sharply. 'The Impalement Arts can involve the throwing of axes, daggers, machetes, arrows, tomahawks—'

'OK, girls, I think we get it,' Stella broke in. 'I presume you're going to be *The Target Twins* now then, since we all know that neither of you can throw for toffee!'

Dulcie and Gemma glared furiously at

Stella before stalking off.

'Those two have always taken themselves far too seriously,' Stella said as she watched them go. She turned to Ava and her dad. 'Well . . . are you going to stay and watch the show this evening?'

Ava's dad shook his head. 'I'm afraid we really must be getting home now.'

'Oh, but you'll come and see us again soon, won't you, Ava?' Lexi asked anxiously.

Ava looked up at her dad, who nodded. 'I'll bring you here myself next time, Ava. Then I can make sure you don't get into any trouble!'

As Stella leaned forward to give Ava a goodbye kiss she said, 'Don't forget your butterfly wings, will you. They're in my caravan. And while you're there you should go and see how pretty you look in my dressing-table mirror.' And she gave Ava a little wink.

Ava kept thinking about that wink all the way to the caravan.

'Dad, Stella can't *know* about the magic mirror, can she?' she asked when she was seated in front of Stella's dressing table looking at her own reflection in the glass.

'Of course she knows,' Dad answered matter-of-factly, helping her on with her wings. 'It would be difficult not to, with us lot coming and going all the time, don't you think?'

Ava was shocked. 'But . . . but she never said anything! Are you sure she knows?'

'Pretty sure, yes.' He gestured with a grin at the bulky dressing table and mirror, which looked so out of place among Stella's other cheerful fifties furnishings. 'I mean, why else would she keep this ugly great thing in her caravan?'

'Oh!' Ava exclaimed, seeing what he meant, and suddenly she was full of questions. But there was no time to ask them, because the mirror was starting to glow and she knew she must keep looking into it, concentrating only on her own reflection, if the magic was to transport her home.

**There are hundreds of beautiful dresses in every
colour of the rainbow — sewn with magic thread.
Take a look, try one on — and wait for the magic
to whisk you away on an amazing adventure!**

Ava is looking for her cat when she finds Marietta's
mysterious shop. She tries on a perfectly fitting gold and
emerald princess dress and whizzes through a secret
mirror — to fairytale land! Will she get there in time
to be a bridesmaid at Cinderella's wedding?

Gwyneth Rees

The Twinkling Tutu

There are hundreds of beautiful dresses in every colour of the rainbow — sewn with magic thread. Take a look, try one on — and wait for the magic to whisk you away on an amazing adventure!

Ava has just discovered the enchantment of Marietta's special dressing-up shop. Now she can't wait to try on a twinkling tutu with matching ballet slippers and pirouette back to Victorian times. Once there she finds she has an important part to play in making a girl's ballerina dreams come true!

A selected list of titles available from Macmillan Children's Books

The prices shown below are correct at the time of going to press. However, Macmillan Publishers reserves the right to show new retail prices on covers, which may differ from those previously advertised.

Gwyneth Rees

The Magic Princess Dress	978-0-330-46113-9	£4.99
The Twinkling Tutu	978-0-330-46116-0	£4.99
Mermaid Magic	978-0-330-42632-9	£5.99
Fairy Dust	978-0-330-41554-5	£5.99
Fairy Treasure	978-0-330-43730-1	£5.99
Fairy Dreams	978-0-330-43476-8	£5.99
Fairy Gold	978-0-330-43938-1	£5.99
Fairy Rescue	978-0-330-43971-8	£5.99
Fairy Secrets	978-0-330-44215-2	£5.99
Cosmo and the Magic Sneeze	978-0-330-43729-5	£5.99
Cosmo and the Great Witch Escape	978-0-330-43733-2	£5.99
Cosmo and the Secret Spell	978-0-330-44216-9	£4.99
Something Secret	978-0-330-46404-8	£5.99

All Pan Macmillan titles can be ordered from our website, www.panmacmillan.com, or from your local bookshop and are also available by post from:

Bookpost, PO Box 29, Douglas, Isle of Man IM99 1BQ

Credit cards accepted. For details:
Telephone: 01624 677237
Fax: 01624 670923
Email: bookshop@enterprise.net
www.bookpost.co.uk

Free postage and packing in the United Kingdom